The Little Duck Who Lost His Quack Quack

By Rick H Drew

Illustrations by Marcos Conde
Edited by Iris Baker

As a child I actually looked forward to bedtime because my mother would tell me some amazing bedtime stories.

My favorite story was "The Little Duck Who Lost his Quack Quack." What made it so much fun to me was each time my mother would reach the words Quack Quack she would pause and I would yell the words Quack Quack out really loud.

That is what will make this story special to your listener. When you reach the words Quack Quack pause and let your listener yell out Quack Quack.

This book is dedicated to my Mother, Doris Singletary Drew, a Southern Belle who was born and raised in a beautiful town in South Georgia called Thomasville.

The forest was waking up, the sun was beginning to glisten on the lake's surface. A Mommy duck and her ducklings lived on the shore. This lake was home to all sorts of animals, birds, and even reptiles.

There was one animal that all of the creatures feared. It was an alligator with some strange eating habits; it only came out to eat in bad weather. On this morning the mommy duck took her babies for a swim. The little ducklings really enjoyed playing and splashing on the water.

They were having so much fun that no one noticed the weather. Suddenly a lightning bolt streaked across the sky, followed by deafening thunder. Mommy duck knew she and her babies were in big trouble. The water was getting rough and difficult to swim in; waves began to crash all around them. Lightning crackled and thunder boomed. Mommy duck headed for shore, her babies followed in single file.

Directly behind the last little duckling a string of bubbles rippled across the surface and then a large grey nostril appeared. The clouds above were on fire as lightening lit up the sky. Without any warning the very last little duckling disappeared with a huge splash.

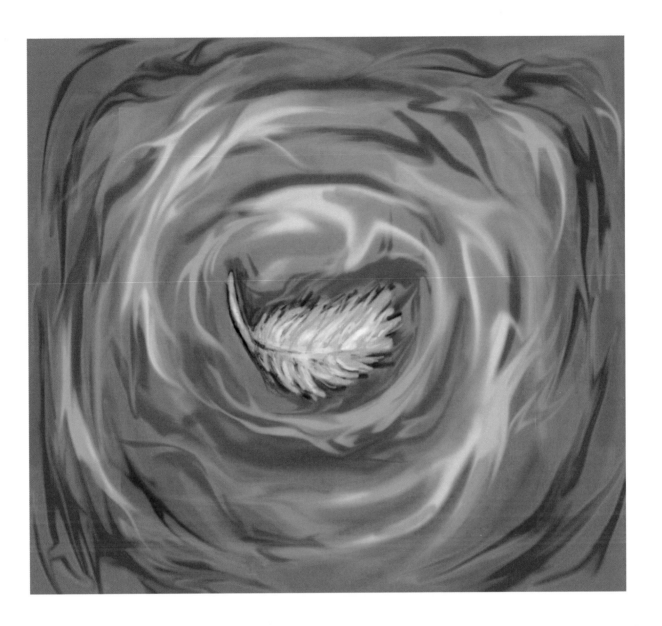

The only thing remaining was a single yellow feather floating on the water's surface. Mommy duck screeched, she knew what happened and she was very sad, but she also knew to save her remaining babies she needed to get to shore quickly.

As she and the others paddled back to shore a miracle happened, the little duckling popped back up to the surface. He was covered with a nasty dark dripping sludge. He gasped for air and was coughing as he tried to catch his breath. He looked around for his Mommy but he was all alone.

He tried to Quack Quack but couldn't, he tried again and again, something awful had happened; this little duck had lost his QUACK QUACK.

Living without his **QUACK QUACK** was just awful. At night he would fall asleep crying and wondering where he had lost it.

One morning he woke up before everyone else and waddled down to the lake. He looked out over the water and wondered where his QUACK QUACK could be.

He would never be happy until he found it so he quietly stepped into the water and began paddling onto the lake.

He was scared, but finding his QUACK QUACK was the most important thing in the world to him.

The little duck looked everywhere, he even looked under floating lily pads.

During his search he paddled up to a tree that had fallen over, some of the branches had fallen into the water.

He heard a strange croaking sound coming from one of the branches just above his head. It was a little green tree frog sunning himself.

The frog looked down at the little duckling staring up at him. He croaked and then asked, "Who are you?"

The little duckling just stared up at him but said nothing.

The frog again asked who he was and what he was looking at. The little duck just shook his head, looked down and began paddling away from the frog.

"I know who you are!" The little frog shouted.

"You're that little duckling that lost his QUACK QUACK, I have heard about you," croaked the frog.

The little duckling nodded his head, looked down again and continued to paddle away.

"Wait a minute maybe I can help you find it," exclaimed the frog.

The little duckling looked back at him with excitement in his eyes. He turned around and paddled back to the frog. The little frog leapt from the tree and landed right on the little duck's back.

"Let's go," said the little frog and off they went in search of the little duck's lost QUACK QUACK.

Meanwhile Mommy duck had been looking all over for her baby. She flew from one side of the lake to the other. Late in the afternoon she landed next to a big brown bear drinking water from the bank. She asked him "Have you seen my baby duckling?"

He growled, looked up at her, then shook his head and continued drinking. After a long day of searching she flew back to her nest.

It was getting dark and the frog suggested they find a safe place to sleep. The duckling paddled to shore where they found a small bush covered with straw.

"This is perfect," said the frog.

"We can sleep under this bush."

Within just a few minutes they were both sound asleep.

The little duckling was startled by the crack of lightning and jumped up from his sleep. It was the first time it had rained since that awful day when he had lost his QUACK QUACK .

"Maybe it's out there right now," he thought, but to look for it in bad weather would be very dangerous.

He looked at his new friend and decided that this part of his journey would have to be done alone, so he stood up quietly and waddled into the night.

The little frog woke up and saw that his new friend was gone. He jumped into the water and began looking for him. The water was rough and difficult to swim in, the frog grew tired quickly.

Just as he turned back to shore, the little duckling who was on top of a wave saw his friend swimming away from him. The little duckling's eyes widened with fear when he saw two huge nostrils peeking through the water's surface. It was the alligator and it was covered with green slime. His huge scaly body followed and it turned slowly in the direction of the little frog.

The large scaly tail swished from one side to the other increasing his speed into the direction of the frog. The alligator was quickly approaching his next meal.

The frog had no idea of the danger just behind him. The little duck tried with all his might to yell for the little frog, but couldn't, he still had not found his QUACK QUACK. The alligator was getting closer with each swish of his tail and his large mouth began to open slowly as he glided through the water. He was now only inches from the exhausted little frog.

The little duck knew if he didn't warn his friend right now he would be eaten by the alligator. All of a sudden he QUACKED out loud. Oh my, he thought, I found it. He quacked as loud as he could.

The little frog heard the quacking and looked back just as two powerful jaws were about to close in on him forever. He jumped as far and hard as any frog has ever jumped; just barely escaping the clamping jaws.

The alligator closed his mouth and disappeared under the dark water. The little frog made it to land dragging his back feet behind him.

Moments later the little duck paddled up to him splashing and quacking. He was very excited that he had found his lost QUACK QUACK.

He was not sure how, nor was he sure where, but he was sure that he had found it. The little frog jumped from the ground onto the little duck's back and thanked him over and over again for saving his life.

At that moment the little duck's Mommy flew over them and landed in the water close by. She was so happy to find her little baby and to see he had found his QUACK QUACK.

The Mommy duck took the little duckling and the frog back to her nest. Everyone was so happy to see the little duckling and to see that he had found his lost QUACK QUACK.

Many years have passed since that horrible day on the lake.

The little duckling was no longer little, he was now a beautiful mallard and the little frog, well; he was still little but much older and wiser.

Today every time dark clouds fill the sky and rain splatters onto the lakes surface, the two friends take off together, the little frog sitting on the duck's back. They patrol the skies around the lake and warn other animals when the alligator surfaces looking for food.

THE END

A NOTE FROM THE AUTHOR

I hope you have enjoyed this story. Having children interact with the reader will keep them interested for a long time.

The imagination is a wonderful thing and reading is the way to jump start the process. Today's children are overwhelmed with technology and video games, but nothing can replace a good book.

Success in school is dependent upon a child's ability to read and comprehend, making reading fun is one of life's greatest gifts

Rick Drew

Made in the USA
Lexington, KY
29 November 2019

57768546R00017